Discover Series
Heavy Equipment

Equipo Pesado

Excavador

Excavator

Make Sure to Check Out the Other Discover Series Books from Xist Publishing:

Published in the United States by Xist Publishing
www.xistpublishing.com
PO Box 61593 Irvine, CA 92602

© 2018 by Xist Publishing All rights reserved
Translated by Victor Santana
No portion of this book may be reproduced without express permission of the publisher
All images licensed from Fotolia
First Bilingual Edition

ISBN: 978-1-5324-0649-2   eISBN: 978-1-5324-0657-7

xist Publishing

Tractor de Granja Completamente Azul

All Blue Farm Tractor

Tractor Rojo

Red Tractor

Tractor de Granja Azul

Blue Farm Tractor

Tractro y Discos

Tractor and Discs

Excavadora Pequeña

Small Excavator

Tractor de Granja Verde

Green Farm Tractor

Motores de Tractor

Tractor Engines

Empujatierra

Bulldozer

Motor de Tractor

Tractor Engine

Tractor Grande Rojo de Granja

Large Red Farm Tractor

Detrás del Tractor de Granja

Back of Farm Tractor

Apisonadora

Roller

Cargadora Pequeña

Small Loader

Tractor Antiguo

Antique Tractor

Retroexcavadora

Backhoe

Tractor Rojo Pequeño

Small Red Tractor

Máquina Elevadora

Forklift

Cargador

Loader

Excavador Amarillo

Yellow Excavator

Cortacésped

Riding Mower

Tractor Agrícola

Farm Tractor

Retroexcavadora

Backhoe

Excavador Grande

Large Excavator

Cargador

Loader

Tractor Verde Antiguo

Green Antique Tractor

Tractor de vía Continua

Continuous Track Tractor

Tractor Viejo

Old Tractor